D0519052

EAST RIDING OF YORKSHIRE
LIBRARY AND
INFORMATION SERVICE
WITHDRAWN FROM STOCK

Please return/renew this item by the last date shown.
Item may also be renewed by the internet*

https://library.eastriding.gov.uk

* Please note a PIN will be required to access this service
- this can be obtained from your library.

Feeling ANGRY!

First published in 2017 by Wayland

Text copyright © Wayland 2017
Illustrations copyright © Mike Gordon 2017

Wayland
Carmelite House
50 Victoria Embankment
London EC4Y 0DZ

Wayland Australia
Level 17/207 Kent Street
Sydney, NSW 2000

Managing editor: Victoria Brooker
Creative design: Paul Cherrill

ISBN: 978 1 5263 0015 7

Printed in China

Wayland is a division of
Hachette Children's Books,
an Hachette UK company.
www.hachette.co.uk

All rights reserved

feeling ANGRY!

Written by
Katie Douglass

Illustrated by
Mike Gordon

WAYLAND

"Aargh, I can't find my bag! Or my keys. And where's my coat?" yelled Harry's dad as he rushed around the lounge.
Harry's dad was late for work.

AGAIN!

"Dad," said Harry, quietly.
"I've got an idea."
"What is it, Harry?"
his dad snapped angrily.

"You're always telling me not to rush about.
If you slow down, maybe that will help?"
suggested Harry.

"Erm, right. Yes, I do say that," Dad said, sheepishly. He stood still, let out a long sigh and looked around. As he did so, he noticed his coat on the back of a chair. His bag was underneath his coat.

"Look," said Harry. "Your keys are here too."
Harry's dad smiled.
"Thanks, Harry. It's hard to stay calm when
you're in a rush. But now I'd really better
get going! See you tonight."

In the kitchen, Harry's sister Susie, was asking for a biscuit.

"For the third time, *no*, Susie! It's time for breakfast. Now please let me get it ready before I lose my temper," said Susie's mum, sounding very much like she'd already lost her temper.

"But I want a biscuit NOW!" Susie shrieked.
Her face was bright red. She looked like
a volcano that had just exploded.

Susie continued to scream.

"Mum, let me try and talk to her," said Harry.

Harry thought that if he could distract Susie, it would stop her thinking about biscuits.

"Susie, look! It's your favourite TV programme."
"Oh, I love this! It's so funny," Susie said,
as she jumped on to the sofa.

Harry breathed a sigh of relief. Now he wouldn't
have to listen to Susie's tantrum any more.

At school, Harry was in the playground when
two of his friends started fighting.
"Oi!" shouted Billy. "Give me back the ball!"
"I was playing with it first!" yelled Charlie.

"No you weren't. I was throwing it to Liam and you just grabbed it. GIVE IT BACK!" Billy raged.
"NO," replied Charlie, fiercely.
Harry really wanted to play ball too, but that wasn't going to happen if his friends kept arguing.

"Hey, you two," Harry interrupted.
"We don't have much playtime
left before class. Don't waste it arguing.
Can't we all play together?"

"Hmm, maybe," Charlie grumbled reluctantly.
"I suppose so," mumbled Billy, looking at his feet.

"Well what are you waiting for?" called Harry.
"Throw Charlie the ball and let's play!"

In class, Harry's friend Lenny was struggling with some maths problems. Lenny was getting more and more frustrated. Harry could see Lenny getting tense and clenching his fists.

Finally, Lenny snapped, crumpled
his bit of paper into a ball
and threw it angrily on the floor.
"I can't do it," he ranted.

"I'm finding the maths hard too," said Harry.
"My mum says, when you're feeling angry,
count to ten and it will help you feel better.
Why don't you try that?"

Lenny thought this sounded like more maths work, but he tried it anyway.

"1, 2, 3, 4 ..."

"5, 6, 7 ..."

"8, 9, 10."

By the time Lenny got to ten, he felt a bit calmer. "It worked!" said Lenny, surprised. "I'll ask Mrs Leroy if she can help us both with this maths problem."

That night, Harry was playing on his tablet.
"Time for bed, Harry," his mum called.
"I just need ten more minutes to
finish this game," he pleaded.

"No, Harry. You've already had ten more minutes."
 "I haven't," Harry argued, without looking up from his tablet.

"Harry, that's enough. Put the tablet down or you'll end up with a ban."
"That's so unfair," Harry shouted and stomped off to his room.

"I think maybe it's time he took some of his own advice," suggested Dad.

Harry was lying face down on his bed, sulking. "Harry," his mum said calmly. "It's time to get ready for bed."

"NO!" shouted Harry angrily.
"Harry, why don't you take some deep
breaths and try to calm down,"
his mum suggested kindly.
"Hmph," grumbled
Harry, still feeling
annoyed.

"Why don't you slowly count to ten?"
Dad said, peering round his door.
Harry sighed irritably.

Susie appeared. "Hey, Harry.
Come to the bathroom. Mum's got you
a new toothbrush," she said, trying to
distract Harry from his mood.

Harry looked from his mum, to his dad, to his sister and couldn't help but smile. They were all using the advice that he'd been giving out today.

"That's all very good advice," he said.
"And I feel much happier now. But...
I still don't want to go to bed!" and he started
bouncing on the bed.

FURTHER INFORMATION

THINGS TO DO

1. Red is a colour that is often linked with anger.

2. This book shows lots of things that people might be angry about, such as school work, bed times and hunger. What other things can you think of that might make people angry?

3. Make a colourful word cloud!
Start with 'angry', then add any other words this makes you think of. Write them all down using different coloured pens. More important words should be bigger, less important words smaller.
Start like this...

RAGE annoyed upset

shout

NOTES FOR PARENTS AND TEACHERS

The aim of this book is to help children think about their feelings
in an enjoyable, interactive way. Encourage them to have fun
pointing to the illustrations, making sounds and acting, too.
Here are more specific ideas for getting more out of the book:

1. Encourage children to talk about their own feelings, if they feel
comfortable doing so, either while you are reading the book or
afterwards. Here are some conversation prompts to try:

What makes you feel angry?
How do you stop feeling angry when this happens?

2. Make a facemask that shows an angry expression.

3. Put on a feelings play! Ask groups of children
to act out the different scenarios in the book.
The children could use their facemasks to
show when they are angry in the play.

4. Hold an angry-face competition. Who can
look the MOST angry?! Strictly no laughing allowed!

BOOKS TO SHARE

A Book of Feelings
by Amanda McCardie, illustrated by Salvatore Rubbino
(Walker, 2016)

Dinosaurs Have Feelings, Too: Anna Angrysaurus
by Brian Moses, illustrated by Mike Gordon
(Wayland, 2015)

I Feel Angry
by Brian Moses, illustrated by Mike Gordon
(Wayland, 1994)

I Hate Everything!
by Sue Graves, illustrated by Desideria Guicciardini
(Franklin Watts, 2014)

The Great Big Book of Feelings
by Mary Hoffman, illustrated by Ros Asquith
(Frances Lincoln, 2016)

Tiger Has a Tantrum (Behaviour Matters)
by Sue Graves, illustrated by Trevor Dunton
(Franklin Watts, 2015)

READ ALL THE BOOKS IN THIS SERIES:

Feeling Angry!
ISBN: 978 1 5263 0015 7

Feeling Frightened!
ISBN: 978 1 5263 0077 5

Feeling Jealous!
ISBN: 978 1 5263 0075 1

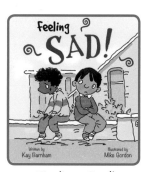

Feeling Sad!
ISBN: 978 1 5263 0071 3

Feeling Shy!
ISBN: 978 1 5263 0079 9

Feeling Worried!
ISBN: 978 1 5263 0073 7